Magic
Animal Friends

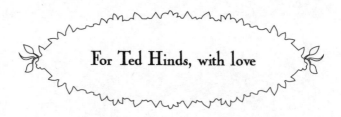

For Ted Hinds, with love

Special thanks to Valerie Wilding

ORCHARD BOOKS

First published in Great Britain in 2017 by The Watts Publishing Group

3 5 7 9 10 8 6 4

Text copyright © Working Partners Ltd 2017
Illustrations copyright © Working Partners Ltd 2017
Series created by Working Partners Ltd

A CIP catalogue record for this book is available from the British Library.

ISBN 978 1 40834 416 3

Printed in Great Britain

MIX
Paper from
responsible sources
FSC® C104740

The paper and board used in this book are made from wood from responsible sources.

Orchard Books
An imprint of Hachette Children's Group
Part of The Watts Publishing Group Limited
Carmelite House, 50 Victoria Embankment, London EC4Y 0DZ

An Hachette UK Company
www.hachette.co.uk
www.hachettechildrens.co.uk

Emma Littleleap
Takes a Chance

Daisy Meadows

ORCHARD

Can you keep a secret? I thought you could!

Then I'll tell you about an enchanted wood.

It lies through the door in the old oak tree,

Let's go there now - just follow me!

We'll find adventure that never ends,

And meet the Magic Animal Friends!

Love,
Goldie the Cat

Contents

CHAPTER ONE

An Exciting Trip

"There! That's the last bit done." With a
swish of her paintbrush, Lily Hart put the
final touches to the words on the sign:

HELPING PAW
WILDLIFE HOSPITAL

Her best friend, Jess Forester, had
painted lots of little animals around the

 9

edge. Both girls adored animals and loved to help out at the wildlife hospital, which Lily's parents ran in a barn at the bottom of their garden.

"Now the sign looks lovely and new again," Jess said.

The girls admired each other's handiwork as Jess's tabby kitten, Pixie, nuzzled their legs.

Lily picked up the kitten. "Look, Pixie!" She laughed. "It's like a typical day in Friendship Forest!"

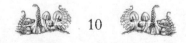

Jess grinned. Friendship Forest was their secret – a magical place where animals lived in little cottages and could talk! The girls' special friend, Goldie the cat, often came to take them there, and together the three of them had had some amazing adventures. The girls always enjoyed meeting their friends at the Toadstool Café, boating down Willowtree River or having a sleepover with Goldie in her grotto.

When Pixie started to squirm in Lily's arms, she gently put the kitten down. She watched as Pixie chased a butterfly behind a rose bush. Lily turned back to Jess, who frowned at the sign. "Something's missing," said Jess.

Lily put her head to one side. "Mmm. It's that empty space below the words. What could go there?"

Suddenly, soft fur brushed against Jess's leg, and she glanced down. A beautiful golden cat with emerald green eyes gazed at her.

"Goldie!" Jess bent down to stroke her

and the cat cuddled up in her arms.

"She's come to take us to Friendship Forest!" said Lily. "We're off on another adventure!"

Goldie darted towards Brightley Stream at the bottom of the garden.

"Let's go!" Lily said. "We'll finish the sign when we get back."

She hurried after Goldie. Both girls knew it didn't matter how long they were away, because time stood still while they were in Friendship Forest.

Jess wiped her brush and popped it in her pocket with the pencil and

 13

sketchbook she always carried. She raced
to catch up to Lily, skipping over the
stepping stones across the stream.

"I hope Grizelda's not causing trouble
on Magic Mountain," Lily panted.

Magic Mountain was the place near
Friendship Forest where all the magic
was made. The animals who lived there
worked together to find crystals, grow
them so they became big and full of
magic, then make those crystals into a
special mixture. Finally, the mixture was
taken to the top of the mountain so it
would rain down everywhere and make

the whole forest magical. A horrible
witch, Grizelda, had already tried to stop
them making the magic so there would
be no magic in Friendship Forest and all
the animals would be forced to leave. The
girls had stopped Grizelda and her troll
servants so far, but they knew the nasty
witch would never give up.

As Goldie reached a dead-looking tree
in the middle of Brightley Meadow, it

 15

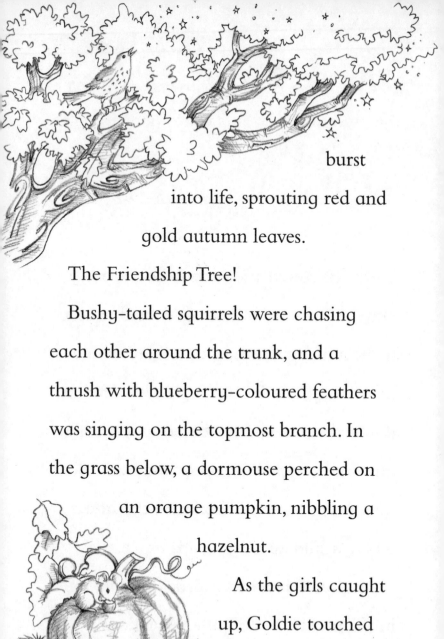

burst into life, sprouting red and gold autumn leaves.

The Friendship Tree!

Bushy-tailed squirrels were chasing each other around the trunk, and a thrush with blueberry-coloured feathers was singing on the topmost branch. In the grass below, a dormouse perched on an orange pumpkin, nibbling a hazelnut.

As the girls caught up, Goldie touched

a paw to the tree, and words appeared in the bark.

Lily and Jess read them aloud: "Friend … ship … For … est!"

Suddenly a small wooden door with a leaf-shaped handle appeared in the trunk. Jess turned the handle and opened the door, letting golden light spill out. They followed Goldie into the shimmering glow and instantly felt the tingle that meant they were shrinking, just a little.

When the light faded, Jess and Lily found themselves in a warm forest glade, lit by autumn sunlight.

 17

There was Goldie, standing as tall as their shoulders. Hugging them, she said, "Welcome back to Friendship Forest."

"It's lovely to be here!" said Jess.

"Is Grizelda up to her old tricks again?" Lily asked.

"We haven't seen her recently," Goldie said. "But someone on Magic Mountain needs your help."

"We're always happy to help the animals of Friendship Forest!' Lily said, and she and Jess followed Goldie to the train that would take them up the magnificent Magic Mountain.

CHAPTER TWO

Up Magic Mountain

The girls were settled in a carriage of the
bright red Friendship Express. The train
wound out of the forest and started up the
snowy track around Magic Mountain.

The girls knew that at every stop lived
a family who helped make the magic
of Friendship Forest. First, the Hoppytail

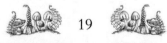

19

family of rabbits dug the crystals out of the ground. Then, the Littlewhiskers chipmunk family grew the crystals in their garden so they were bigger. The last two families lived even higher on the mountain but the girls hadn't met them yet.

As they passed the Hoppytail house, the little bunnies all waved and the girls blew kisses back, especially to their friend, Pippa Hoppytail.

Something tickled around their necks.

Lily reached to her collar and felt a necklace there.

"Our pendants are back now we're on the mountain!" Lily cried.

Pippa had given magical pendants to each of the friends. Goldie's blue one made things change colour. Jess's pink one made things change shape, and Lily's white pendant made things disappear.

Jess looked at her pendant as it twinkled in the light.

Mr Whistlenose, the driver, stopped the

train at Fluffywhiskers Garden. The girls could see the chipmunk family scurrying around their garden.

Ranger Tuftybeard, the big white goat who carried the magic crystals up the mountain, climbed on to the train, holding a backpack full of the glowing rocks.

"Hello, Lily and Jess!" he said, "Lovely to see you. Where are you off to today?"

"I'm taking them to meet the Littleleap

family," said Goldie.

The ranger beamed, "That's where I'm going too! They're my cousins."

Ranger Tuftybeard explained that when the Fluffywhiskerses' crystals were fully grown and dug up from the ground, he took them up to the Littleleaps. "Their magical swizzle stick dissolves the crystals into a mixture called Magic Mist. It's this Magic Mist that makes all the magic in Friendship Forest."

"We need magic to get through the Friendship Tree," said Lily. "Imagine! Without it we could never come here, and

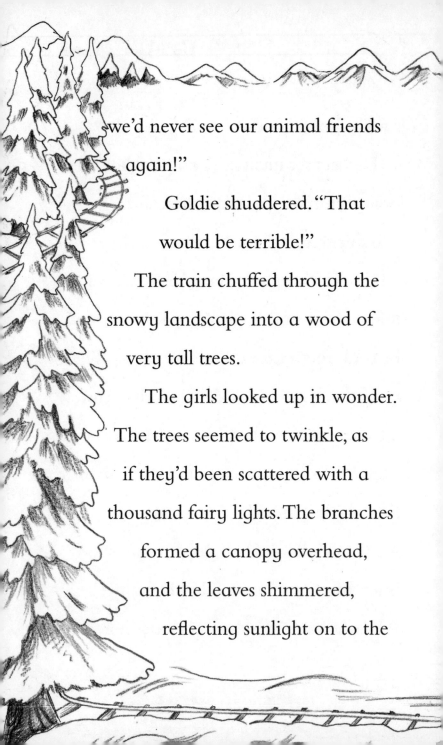

we'd never see our animal friends
again!"

Goldie shuddered. "That
would be terrible!"

The train chuffed through the
snowy landscape into a wood of
very tall trees.

The girls looked up in wonder.
The trees seemed to twinkle, as
if they'd been scattered with a
thousand fairy lights. The branches
formed a canopy overhead,
and the leaves shimmered,
reflecting sunlight on to the

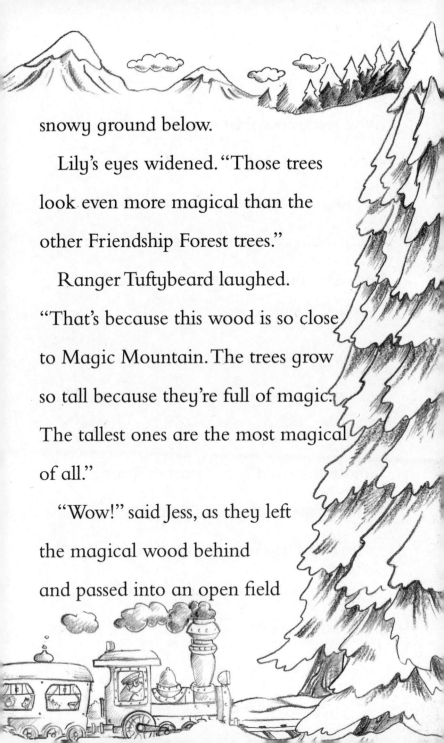

snowy ground below.

Lily's eyes widened. "Those trees look even more magical than the other Friendship Forest trees."

Ranger Tuftybeard laughed. "That's because this wood is so close to Magic Mountain. The trees grow so tall because they're full of magic. The tallest ones are the most magical of all."

"Wow!" said Jess, as they left the magical wood behind and passed into an open field filled with powdery snow.

"Nearly there!" said Goldie. "It's cold outside, so I've brought some Winter Warmers." She lifted a lid in the arm of her seat and took out three red flowers with sparkling centres.

The girls knew that if they wore one, it would keep their whole body warm. They tucked the flowers into their hair, and Goldie fastened hers into her scarf.

The train halted at a station called Littleleap Crossing. Jess and Lily stepped out, gazing around at a world of snowdrifts, ice and deep blue sky. The pale sun warmed their cheeks and glittered off the crisp white snow.

Ranger Tuftybeard lifted three sacks out of the train. "Would you give me a hand carrying these here crystals?" he asked.

"Of course!" said Lily.

Ranger Tuftybeard and the girls heaved the sacks on to their shoulders, and Goldie led them up a snowy track.

As they walked along the path, the little group passed wonderful snow sculptures. There was a tree, a bench and a stunning bush covered in flowers.

"Wow!" cried Jess.

"Look!" Lily gasped. "Animals!"

They passed a fox, an eagle, a penguin and a row of bunnies – all made of snow.

"I wish I could do that!" Jess said.

Moments later, Goldie stopped before a cave with 'Littleleap Lodge' painted above its pretty, rounded blue door. She knocked.

There was the sudden clatter of feet.

For a moment Lily felt frightened. "It sounds like an avalanche!"

Goldie grinned. "It is, in a way. Here come the Littleleaps!"

CHAPTER THREE

Nasty Visitors

The door opened and the girls were instantly surrounded by three prancing, dancing, excited goat kids.

"Little ones!" said Mrs Littleleap, wrapping a fluffy red shawl around her shoulders. "I'm sure our visitors would like to come inside for some hot chocolate."

 29

"Yes, please!" said Lily and Jess.

A kid in a striped T-shirt, and another wearing a feather boa, scurried indoors.

The oldest, a golden-brown kid with a snowflake-patterned scarf, slipped her tiny hoof into Jess's hand. "I'm Emma," she said. "My brother's Pip and my sister's Lavender."

She took them into a cosy sitting room where squishy sofas stood before a crackling log fire. Toys littered the rug.

Goldie sat beside Emma. She turned towards the girls. "Emma is an amazing artist!" she beamed.

The kid's pink nose turned an even deeper pink.

"And she's having an art display tonight," said Goldie.

"That's great!" cried Jess.

"Hmm," said Emma, looking uncertain.

"What's wrong?" asked Lily. "Aren't you excited?"

 31

"I am. It's just ..."

Mrs Littleleap shook her head sadly.
"I'm afraid Mr Littleleap isn't here," she

said. "He's the best at
calming Emma when
she gets nervous. But
he's away down in
the forest today."

Emma frowned.
"Suppose my work's
not good enough?"

"She heard from Goldie that Jess is a
talented artist," Mrs Littleleap explained.
"We think if she hears you say her work's

good, she'll be happier."

Jess smiled. "I'm sure your art is wonderful. Can we see some of it?"

Emma looked puzzled. "Haven't you already?"

The girls shook their heads.

"Didn't you notice the sculptures beside the path?" asked Emma.

Lily gasped. "You did those? They're amazing!"

"You're a fantastic artist!" said Jess.

Emma stared, open-mouthed. "Do you really think so?"

Mrs Littleleap tutted. "I told you,

33

Emma. Your art is beautiful. You should believe in yourself. Isn't that right, Ranger Tuftybeard?"

"Couldn't agree more," he said, doffing his hat.

Emma sighed sadly. "I was hoping my dad would be here to support me, but I don't know if he'll be back in time."

Mrs Littleleap smiled and said, "I've got to make some more Magic Mist. Even on the day of the art display, we all have to do our jobs!"

Lily jumped up. "Can we help?"

"Yes, please!" said Emma and her mum.

Jess and Lily carried the sacks of crystals into a small, white-painted room. A huge white bowl stood on a table.

Mrs Littleleap took a large swizzle stick – like a big wooden spoon – from a white shelf.

The girls gasped. The swizzle stick was a brilliant blaze of colour. It was painted with a beautiful pattern in vivid shades of red, gold, sky blue, sea green and plum.

"That's so lovely," said Jess.

"That's because it's made from the deepest, oldest magic in Friendship Forest," said Mrs Littleleap. "When we

35

stir the crystals with it …" She dropped a few of the crystals into the white bowl. "… they dissolve and create Magic Mist." A puff of glittery steam rose from the bowl. "Just like this—"

There was a sudden thump on the door.

"Who can that be?" said Mrs Littleleap, going to answer it. "It's too early for the

display, but maybe someone couldn't wait." She hurried to the door with the swizzle stick still in her hand.

The friends followed her to see who had arrived. Before they reached the door, it burst open.

There stood a tall, bony figure with green hair swirling around her head like snapping snakes. She wore a purple tunic over skinny black trousers, and high-heeled boots with sharply pointed toes.

"Grizelda!" cried Lily.

"Go away, you mean witch!" said Jess.

The witch barged inside. To the girls'

 37

dismay, Grizelda's four trolls followed.

Rocky's long tongue flopped sideways
and Flinty's sticking-out ears waggled
as she grinned, showing gappy teeth.
Pebble's long nose wobbled and Craggy
shuffled around on his knobbly grey feet.
The greedy trolls did whatever Grizelda
wanted, because she'd promised them an

enormous feast if they helped her ruin the
Friendship Forest magic.

Now they surrounded Mrs Littleleap,
who dropped the swizzle stick in fright.

Grizelda shoved Rocky. "Out of my
way!" she snapped, grabbing at the
swizzle stick.

"No!" Emma cried. She leapt between
the trolls' hairy knees, snatched the swizzle
stick up from the floor and ran behind Jess
and Lily.

"You're not getting that swizzle stick,
Grizelda!" Lily yelled.

"I am!" the witch snarled. "No one

 39

will make magic with it ever again. The
animals will have to leave. Friendship
Forest will be MINE!"

She pointed a bony finger at Emma
and screeched, "Get that swizzle stick!"

The trolls circled around, trying to
reach the little kid. But Emma ducked
round them and dashed outside, clutching
the swizzle stick in her mouth. The girls
and Goldie raced after her, slamming the
door behind them.

CHAPTER FOUR

The Trolls
Give Chase!

Goldie and the girls slipped from side to side on the icy path.

Emma's hooves click-clacked as she called, "This way!"

Lily glanced back. The trolls were close behind them.

 41

Emma turned on to a narrow track that sloped downhill. The others followed but the closer they got to a deep ravine between two icy cliffs, the more nervous the girls became.

"Emma, should we turn around?" Jess asked, her voice trembling.

"This cliff is steep!" Lily added.

But Emma galloped right up to the edge of the cliff and leapt across the ravine, landing on a ledge below.

The girls and Goldie slid to a stop.

Emma tucked the swizzle stick into her scarf. "Jump!" she called. "The magic of

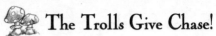
the mountain won't let

you fall."

"Emma knows the

mountain," said Lily. "We

should trust her."

"OK," Jess said shakily.

"Emma's mum told her she

should believe in herself. We

should believe in ourselves too."

"I'll go first," Goldie said.

Taking a deep

breath, she

backed up

a few

paces then raced towards the cliff edge. At the last moment, she leapt across, landing safely on the far side.

Just then Lily heard the trolls arguing loudly.

"Girls go that way!" Flinty grunted.

"Flinty stupid," rasped Rocky. "That way."

Suddenly, Pebble shrieked and pointed. "There! Girls!"

Jess grasped Lily's hand. "They've seen

us. Let's jump together."

Lily nodded, and they took a few steps back then ran straight for the cliff edge.

"Now!" cried Jess, and they sailed over the ravine. They felt the magic of the mountain carrying them safely across. They landed, rolling straight into Goldie, who hugged them tightly. "You're so brave!" she said.

Emma bleated in alarm. "The trolls are coming," she said. "We must get to the next clifftop."

With the swizzle stick peeking out of the top of her scarf, she leapt from icy ledge to icy ledge.

As Goldie and the girls followed, Jess glanced back. To her dismay, she saw Rocky reach the cliff. He hesitated at the size of the gap but, just as they had, he took a few steps back then ran and

leapt, sailing across the ravine with ease. The moment he landed on the other side he started running again.

"They're catching up!" Jess yelled.

Emma picked up the pace, Lily, Jess and Goldie following as quickly as they could. The trolls weren't far behind. They felt the ground shake each time a troll jumped to another ledge, sending stones rattling down, down, down into the ravine.

Emma called back, "Don't look down. Look ahead. Watch where you're jumping to, and you'll land safely!"

Jess was astonished. "She's so unsure

about her artwork, but so confident on the mountain!"

"Those trolls don't look confident." Lily looked back at the trolls, pleased to see them pausing at the next cliff edge. The distance between the cliffs was getting larger.

"Me scared," shouted Flinty, her ears flapping in the wind.

"Trolls get swizzle stick!" said Rocky.

Pebble nodded. "Then witch give trolls big feast."

"Om-nom-nom!" said Craggy. "Trolls go faster!"

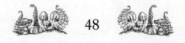

The Trolls Give Chase!

Together, the trolls crouched then
jumped for the next cliff. As soon as they
landed they started to run.

"Hurry!" cried Jess. "They're gaining on
us!"

Since the trolls could take big steps,
it wasn't long before Craggy was close
enough to grab Goldie and the girls.

He reached out for them, but they
wriggled out of his grasp and leapt to
the next ledge. Jess and Lily scrambled on
to another one but, behind them, Goldie
cried out.

They looked back. She had landed

 49

safely, but her
paw had become
lodged in a crack
between the rocks.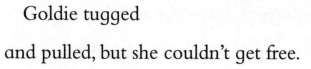

"Hang on,
Goldie!" Lily
yelled.

Goldie tugged
and pulled, but she couldn't get free.

"We're coming!" Jess shouted, slithering
towards her.

The trolls laughed.

"Cat is stuck!" Rocky sniggered. "We
got you now."

"No, you don't!" Lily shouted. "If you trolls come near, I'll – I'll knock you over!" She threw handfuls of snow at them, giving Emma and Jess time to grab Goldie's paws.

"All right," Jess panted. "On three, Emma. One … two … three … pull!"

While they pulled, Lily flung more snow at the trolls. "Get away!"

"Ach!" Craggy shouted, as wet snow ran down his front. "Trolls not like wet."

"Too bad!" yelled Lily. "Have some more!" She hurled more and more snowballs, which hit the trolls in the face.

"Ow!" cried
Pebble.

Flinty and Rocky
wiped snow from
their faces and
shuddered. "Brr ...
cold, cold, cold!"

Goldie's paw was
nearly out. Just a few
seconds more and she'd be free.

"Last tug," Jess said. "Heave!"

With a great popping sound, Goldie's
paw came out of the hole in the rock.
But as Goldie tumbled into Emma, the

kid lost her balance and the swizzle stick
went flying out of her scarf.

The girls watched it slide towards the
edge. Then … over it went!

"Oh no!" cried Emma.

The friends peered into the ravine. Down, down, down the swizzle stick tumbled. It smashed against a rock and shattered into pieces.

Emma burst into tears.

CHAPTER FIVE

A Difficult Task

Jess and Lily couldn't stop Emma crying.

"I'm so sorry," she sobbed.

"It's not your fault," said Jess.

"No, it's those mean old trolls," said Lily.

Next to them, the trolls were arguing

noisily.

"Swizzle stick gone!"

 55

"Swizzle stick broke!"

"Ergh! What trolls do now?"

Lily ignored them. "You did brilliantly, Emma," she said firmly. "You dropped the swizzle stick because you saved Goldie."

"But we can't dissolve the crystals now," Emma wept. "You know what will happen to the forest when the magic runs out."

The girls nodded. Without magic, all the things that made Friendship Forest so safe and special would disappear, and Grizelda would make it dark and scary. The animals would have to leave and find somewhere new to live.

Goldie looked worried, too. "If the magic stops, you girls won't be able to visit us ever again."

Everyone grew quiet, tears welling in their eyes. No one could bear the thought of Lily and Jess never being able to come back.

"We must make sure that the magic doesn't stop," Lily said firmly.

"How?" asked Emma.

Lily hugged her, thinking desperately. Finally, she said, "I've got it! We'll make another swizzle stick!"

 57

The trolls laughed loudly. Rocky's long tongue flopped about as he chortled, "Girls make swizzle stick. Trolls steal it!"

The trolls stomped away up the steep slope, still laughing.

"Do you know if it's even possible?" asked Jess.

"We'll ask Ranger Tuftybeard," said Goldie. "He knows everything about Magic Mountain."

The friends set off towards Emma's

house, hoping that the ranger would know how to make another magical swizzle stick. It was their only chance.

At Littleleap Lodge, they found Ranger Tuftybeard drinking jasmine tea and comforting a worried Mrs Littleleap. There was no sign of Grizelda.

Mrs Littleleap cuddled Emma. "Thank goodness you're safe!" she said. "What happened?"

Jess explained what had happened and how the swizzle stick had broken.

"I'm so sorry, Mum," Emma

whimpered. "I've let you and Dad down."

Mrs Littleleap kissed Emma's tiny pink nose. "You have never let us down," she soothed. "And together we'll figure out what to do about the swizzle stick."

"Is it possible to make a new one?" Lily asked.

Ranger Tuftybeard scratched one of his horns. "Hmm," he said. "It *is* possible ..."

"Hooray!" the friends cried.

"… but it will be difficult," he continued. "You need wood from a very magical tree. It must be carved in a very particular shape. Finally, it must be painted with a very special design – using magical paint."

Lily glanced at Jess, who nodded. "It might be tough," she said, "but with Emma's help, I'm sure we can do it."

Goldie hugged the girls. "When we need help, you never let us down," she said.

"Where do we start?" Lily wondered.

"Wood from a very magical tree
…" Jess said slowly. "What about those
twinkling trees we passed on the train?"

"They're the most magical ones I
know," Ranger Tuftybeard replied.

"I know how we can get there fast!"
Emma cried as she led them outside. "Wait
here." She disappeared around the side of
the cave.

Moments later, she returned, pulling a
sledge with "Leap-A-Lots" painted along
the side. "This will whizz us down the
mountain in no time," she said. "Jump on!"

Goldie and the girls sat behind Emma.

Soon the girls' hair was flying and the
wind whistled past their ears as they
zoomed downhill.

Emma followed the path down into
the magical forest, steering the sledge
carefully around sharp bends.

The girls and Goldie clutched each other as they swerved from side to side.

Jess and Lily whooped. This sledge ride was great fun!

Soon, the ground levelled out and they slid to a stop. The four friends all jumped off.

Tall trees stood all around. The canopy of branches overhead twinkled and sparkled silver and gold, reflecting shimmering light on the snow below. It looked as if hundreds of fireflies were dancing around the friends.

A twinkling leaf drifted down, as bright

as if it had been dipped in sunshine.

Lily grinned. "This is definitely a very magical wood!"

CHAPTER SIX

Clever Emma!

"Remember," said Jess, "Ranger Tuftybeard said the tallest trees are the most magical."

Emma skipped ahead, full of bounce. Soon she stopped in the middle of a ring of trees. "These are the tallest."

The girls looked up. One tree was taller

 67

than the rest. It
seemed to reach for
the clouds. Its dancing
leaves twinkled more brightly
than the others, and the air
around it seemed to hum.

"This tree must be the most
magical of all!" Lily said.

Goldie climbed up the tree
trunk and reached for a branch.
Before she'd even touched it, the
branch snapped off and dropped
into her paws.

The girls were astonished.

"It knows what we need!" said Lily.

Goldie jumped down and Jess took the branch from her. "This must be right for the new swizzle stick."

Taking turns to pull the sledge, they set off up the mountain. They had the wood they needed – now they had to carve it into a perfectly shaped swizzle stick.

Ranger Tuftybeard admired the branch. "Oh, 'tis perfect," he said.

"Who made the old swizzle stick?" Lily asked the ranger.

"My great-great-grandfather," he said.

Jess smiled. "Then you should make the new one."

He coughed. "I'm no artist. I couldn't do it. Not properly."

Jess said anxiously, "But if it's not made correctly, it might not work."

After a moment's thought, the girls grinned at each other. They had both had the same idea!

"Emma!" said Lily. "You can do it!"

"Me?" said Emma.

"Of course!" said Jess. "You're a fantastic sculptor!"

The kid looked unsure. "Do you really think I could?"

Everyone said, "Yes!"

"Suppose it's not good enough?" Emma said nervously.

Mrs Littleleap kissed her cheek. "Believe in yourself."

Emma fetched her tools and soon she was whittling away at the branch from the magical tree.

"The swizzle stick needs to be just the right size," Ranger Tuftybeard told her. "As long as a cat's tail, as wide as a goat's beard, and as smooth as a kid's hoof."

Everyone watched, fascinated, as chips of wood flew beneath Emma's busy little hooves. Every so often, she paused to check the length against Goldie's tail and the width against Ranger Tuftybeard's beard.

She started cutting curves into

the wood and the girls watched it become

swizzle stick-shaped. Next, Emma scraped,

rubbed and polished until the wood

gleamed as brightly as her own little

hooves in the firelight.

Finally, she held up the swizzle stick,

asking nervously, "What do you think?"

"Perfect!" said Mrs Littleleap.

"Well done!" cried Goldie and Lily.

Jess hugged her. "You're an excellent

artist!"

Emma's pale pink nose turned bright

pink.

Ranger Tuftybeard examined the

swizzle stick. "'Tis marvellous!" he said. "Now we must make the special paint."

Mrs Littleleap gave baskets to Emma, Goldie and the girls, and they followed Ranger Tuftybeard outside.

"We need berries from the rainbow briar," he said, pointing to a rambling bush lower down the mountain. Heavy bunches of different-coloured berries hung from it, shimmering like soap bubbles in the sunlight.

"The berries ooze brightly coloured juice when you squeeze them," Ranger

Tuftybeard explained.

The friends wasted no time and headed down the sculpture path to the rainbow briar. The berries were all kinds of different colours – not just blue, red or yellow! There were different shades of blue, from sky blue to purple, and every shade of red from shell pink to deep crimson. Yellows shaded from pale banana to deepest orange.

Jess touched an indigo berry. "It feels velvety," she said, and squeezed it. Deep bluey-violet juice ran out. "It's like squeezing a tube of paint!"

Everyone quickly picked as many berries as they could, until they couldn't fit any more in their baskets.

They headed back to Littleleap Lodge clutching their brimming baskets. Halfway there, Jess heard a deep, far-off rumbling.

She glanced back down the mountain. "The trolls!" she cried.

Rocky and the others were barging through the trees below.

"Hurry!" Lily cried. "They're coming this way!"

CHAPTER SEVEN

Magical Paint

Emma hurried past her snow sculptures. The others were slower – they weren't used to running in the snow and ice.

"The trolls are catching up," Jess panted. "We'll never make it!"

"I've got an idea," Lily gasped. "Let's disguise ourselves as snow creatures and

77

stand beside Emma's sculptures!"

"Of course!" Jess said. "Our magical pendants!"

Emma looked puzzled. "What magical pendants?"

Lily pulled out her white pendant. "Mine makes things vanish."

Jess showed Emma her pink pendant. "This changes things into the shape of something else, like a disguise."

"Mine changes colours," said Goldie.

"Could you use yours to turn us snow white?" Lily asked hurriedly. "Then Jess can use her pendant to disguise us as sculptures. Hurry! The trolls are coming!"

After they hid their baskets full of berries in a nearby snowdrift, Goldie concentrated on her pendant.

The girls felt as if butterfly wings were fluttering over them as their clothes, skin and hair turned completely white.

"My turn," said Jess. "Each of you stand beside an animal sculpture." She concentrated on her pendant.

Shivers ran through the girls, like rippling waves.

Jess grinned as she looked over at Lily: she was now a snow-white squirrel!

They'd all changed. Jess was a fox and
Emma and Goldie were
two owls.

The girls held
their breath as the
trolls appeared, with
wheezy gasps and
pounding feet.

Craggy flopped on
to the snow bench,
which collapsed. "Need rest!"

Lily and Jess held their breath.

Pebble and Rocky grunted in
agreement but Flinty flapped her ears and

said, "Trolls follow girls. Now! Make sure
not got new swizzle stick."

"OK. Find girls,"
said Craggy.
He got up and
followed the
others, his
knobbly grey
feet slapping
the path as he
headed uphill.

The trolls had just rounded the corner
when Jess saw that she'd completely
transformed back into her real self.

"Phew! They left in the nick of time," said Jess.

"The magic lasted just long enough," said Goldie, as her white fur turned back to gold.

"Hoot!" said Emma. "Hoot!"

The others stared in dismay.

"She's still part owl!" Lily said.

Emma giggled. "Just kidding!"

Everyone laughed as they dug their baskets of berries out of the snowdrift and set off up the hill.

Back at the cave, Mrs Littleleap had her biggest pot ready for the berries.

"This belonged to Emma's great-great-grandmother," she said. "She mixed paint for Ranger Tuftybeard's great-great-grandfather."

"'Tis perfect!" said Ranger Tuftybeard. "Emma, could you do a design for the swizzle stick?"

Emma hesitated, so Jess said quickly, "Can I help?"

"Yes, please!" said Emma.

Jess took out her little sketchbook. "Let's draw some designs in here."

The others watched Ranger Tuftybeard squeeze some plump pink berries into the

 83

bowl. He added a little magic mist from the white bowl Mrs Littleleap had used earlier, and glitter from Emma's craft box.

The berry juice swished around the pot by itself, then sent up a puff of pink sparkles.

"It's ready!" said Ranger Tuftybeard. He poured the pink paint into a dish. "Lily, why don't you make some blue paint?"

Lily squeezed the velvety berries, added the magical mist and glitter, and soon a puff of sapphire blue sparkles twinkled above the bowl.

 85

Goldie made emerald green paint, Mrs Littleleap made purple, then they took turns mixing different colours until Emma waved Jess's sketchbook, crying, "Ready!"

Everyone looked at Emma's sketches and admired the design of trailing leaves weaving between flowers. The bowl of the swizzle stick would have tiny stars and moons on a midnight blue background.

"Magical!" they all agreed.

Ranger Tuftybeard offered Emma a brush. "Magic Mountain's most gifted artist should paint the swizzle stick."

Emma clutched Jess's hand, smiling.

"I'm not the only artist," she said. "We'll do it together."

Jess fished in her pocket for the brush she'd used at Helping Paw, and dipped it into a bowl of vivid green paint. "I'll paint the leaves."

Emma chose scarlet, purple and gold for the flowers and put a brush beside each bowl. "Scarlet first," she said, and set to work.

Ranger Tuftybeard dozed by the fire. Mrs Littleleap got busy cooking, with Pip and Lavender helping. Lily and Goldie kept watch for the trolls, who they knew

 87

would still be on the mountain looking for them. Lily could hear their thundering footsteps nearby. She began to laugh. "Silly trolls," she said. "They have no idea where we are!"

"I bet they're following our old footprints!" Goldie laughed along with them.

Ranger Tuftybeard gave a great snort and woke himself up. "Who? What?" he mumbled.

Everyone giggled, and soon the ranger joined in. "How is the swizzle stick coming along?" he asked finally.

"Almost finished. I hope it's OK,"
Emma said anxiously, as she put the
last dab of paint on the swizzle stick.
Suddenly, the colours shone as brilliantly
as sparks from a diamond, and the stars in
the bowl of the swizzle stick twinkled like
stars in the night sky.

"By my beard!" said Ranger

Tuftybeard, examining

the swizzle stick

closely. He

peered at it from this way and that. At last, he lifted it and said. "Perfect! I can actually feel the magic."

Jess and Emma clasped hands and hooves and danced around, singing, "We made a magic swizz-wizz-wizz-le stick!"

"Emma's a wonderful artist!" chanted Lily and Goldie.

Mrs Littleleap smiled. "Emma," she said. "Surely you can believe in yourself now!"

The kid's pale pink nose turned as red as a cherry! "I think I can."

CHAPTER EIGHT

A Wonderful Surprise

As the friends celebrated, Lily glanced
outside. An orb of yellow-green light was
floating towards them.

"Oh no!" she cried. "Grizelda!"

The trolls must have seen it too because
they ran over. The witch glared at the
trolls, green hair whipping round her face.

 91

The trolls cowered as she shook her fists,
screeching, "You lazy fools. You couldn't
steal a teensy little swizzle stick!"

Rocky looked up. "Stick big, not little!"

"Don't argue!" Grizelda screamed. "I
could have taken control of Friendship
Forest. But you failed me. You're useless!"

As she turned her gaze on the faces at the window, the trolls scuttled away.

"You pesky girls and that mangy cat might have stopped my plan," she shrieked at them through the glass, "but I'll be back! You'll never win!"

When she spun around and realised the trolls had fled down the hill, she screamed in fury and stormed after them.

The friends breathed sighs of relief as the witch disappeared.

"Grizelda's the one who will never win," said Goldie. "Not while Jess and Lily are around!"

"Goodness!" said Mrs Littleleap. "It'll soon be time for the show. I must make enough Magic Mist to fire up the train!"

She dropped handfuls of the sparkling crystals into the bowl.

"It's working!" cried Lily, as a cloud of pink steam formed above the bowl.

Mrs Littleleap smiled. "The magic is made!" Everyone cheered. Friendship Forest would not run out of magic today!

Soon enough, it was time for Emma's display. Entering the ice cave, they saw her colourful paintings, bright against the white walls. A table was laden with Mrs Littleleap's delicious snacks and drinks.

The girls waited outside with Emma. She looked excited, but anxious.

"Are you still worried about people seeing your display?" Jess asked.

"You can't really still think you're not good enough, surely?" said Lily. "Not after what you've done today!"

"No," said Emma. "I really do believe in myself at last! Now I'm worried that no one will come." Tears filled her eyes. "I wish Dad was here. He always makes me feel better."

Jess hugged her. "I'm sure everyone—"

Peeep!

"The train!" Lily cried.

The whistle blew as Mr Whistlenose drove into Littleleap Crossing.

A few minutes later, a crowd of animals appeared along the sculpture path.

"We're so excited!" cried Mrs Twinkletail the mouse, pulling her ten children along on a sled train.

"So are we!" squealed the Fluffytails.

Lots and lots of animals followed. Last of all came someone who made Emma squeal in delight.

"Dad!"

Emma Littleleap did a great big leap –
towards the billy goat.

"I thought you had important work to
do," Emma said.

"I did! I had to make sure our friends
made it to my little kid's first art display,"
Mr Littleleap said in a gruff voice. "That's
where I've been, spreading the word.

Everyone wanted to come!"

Emma hugged him with all her might.

They went into the cave and found

everyone admiring the pretty paintings

and enjoying Mrs Littleleap's fruit tarts

and sparkleberry fizz. Lots of animals

asked Emma to do paintings for them.

Before long, it was time for the girls to

leave. They said goodbye to everyone, and

gave a beaming Emma a special hug.

"It's a wonderful display," said Jess.

Lily nodded. "We're all proud of you."

"Especially us!" said Mrs Littleleap.

Emma's dad scooped her up. "I'm so happy I made it tonight," he said. "Thank you, girls, for being such good friends, and defeating Grizelda for us."

"We couldn't have done it without Emma's talent," said Jess.

"Or her confidence," Lily added.

"We must go," said Goldie.

"Bye!" the girls cried, as the animals waved them off.

"Bye, Jess and Lily!" called the animals.
"Come back soon!"

Goldie touched the Friendship Tree, and
a door opened in the trunk, spilling out
golden light.

She hugged the girls.
"Grizelda would
have taken over
the forest by
now if you
hadn't helped."

"We're always
ready to help

Friendship Forest," said Lily. "Whenever we're needed! Bye, Goldie."

The girls stepped into the golden glow and felt a tingle as they returned to their proper size. When the light faded, they were in Brightley Meadow.

They skipped back to Helping Paw, chatting excitedly about their adventure. As they got nearer to the barn, little Pixie scampered to meet them.

Lily picked her up for a cuddle and saw the sign they'd been painting before they left. The paint was still wet, of course.

"It still needs something to finish it off,

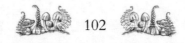

Jess," Lily said. "See if there's anything in your sketchbook to inspire you."

Jess flicked through the pages, then stared. "I didn't do this." She showed Lily a design of two paws touching each other. "It must have been Emma! I've got an idea ..." She took Pixie from Lily and dipped her paw pad in some amber paint. Then she gently touched the kitten's paw to the sign, twice.

Pixie purred as Lily cleaned her paw, then the girls stood back, admiring their sign. Below the words 'Helping Paw', Jess had dabbed two paw prints, overlapping.

They made a
heart shape.

"A paw-print
heart is the perfect finish," said Lily.
"Our sign shows what Helping Paw is all
about."

"Yes," said Jess, "love for animals!"

As the paint dried in the sun, the girls
watched Pixie chase another butterfly
through the garden. They giggled as the
kitten balanced on the rocks surrounding
the pond, leaping from stone to stone, just
like a little goat kid they knew.

The End

Wicked witch Grizelda is still trying to ruin the magic of Friendship Forest. Can little white fox Sarah Scramblepaw help save the day?

Find out in Lily and Jess's next adventure,

Sarah Scramblepaw's Big Step

Turn over for a sneak peek ...

"It's raining cats and dogs out there!" said Lily Hart, pulling on a pair of wellies by the back door of her kitchen. "We'd better help take the animals inside."

"Good idea," said Lily's best friend, Jess Forester. She picked up an umbrella with wide red and yellow stripes and together the girls hurried out into the downpour, sheltering under Jess's umbrella.

In the garden, the animals of Helping Paw Wildlife Hospital were huddled up inside their hutches. Lily's parents had set up the hospital, and she and Jess loved to help out whenever they could. Mr and

Mrs Hart were already gathering up the bunnies, guinea pigs and hedgehogs to take indoors.

"Can you girls take the fox cubs in?" Mrs Hart called. "They're being a bit of a handful!"

She pointed to an open-air pen, where some little fox cubs were wrestling and rolling on the muddy ground. They were soaked!

Jess unbolted the gate and Lily stepped into the pen. She bent down to scoop up a fox cub. But the little creature scurried away from her, waving his bushy tail.

"I think they're enjoying it!" said Jess, laughing as another tiny fox cub squirmed out of her hands and jumped into a puddle with a splash.

Soon the girls had rounded up all the wriggling little foxes and carried them into the warm barn. As they went back outside again, a golden cat with green eyes that matched the wet grass ran towards them.

"Goldie!" said Lily and Jess at the same time.

Their special cat friend let out a soft purr in reply.

Jess gasped. "You know what this means," she said. "We're going to Friendship Forest!"

Read

Sarah Scramblepaw's Big Step

to find out what happens next!